The Adventures of Granny Lane

By
June Soo

The Adventures of Granny Lane: ©June Soo 2021.
First Edition: ©June Soo 2021
Cover Design: ©June Soo & Beatles Liverpool and More Ltd.
Editor: June Soo.
Publisher: Beatles Liverpool and More Ltd.
ISBN: 978-1-8381238-1-9

The Adventures of Granny Lane:

This is a humorous story of Louise, who in her early 70s finds herself retired and widowed.

Having downsized her home she wakes up on Christmas Day admitting to herself that she is lonely and realising that she must do something about it.

Already a lover of challenges and projects, as she calls them, she unexpectedly finds herself propelled into another world where she meets people from all walks of life who like her need an aim in life but above all friendship.

Granny Lane's Christmas

CHAPTERS

1. *"Life is not a rehearsal, live it."* **10**

2. *"Believe you can and you're halfway there." Theodore Roosevelt.* **13**

3. *"A book is like a garden in your pocket" Chinese Proverb.* **17**

4. *"Love, Laugh and Live."* **21**

5. *"Only a life lived for others is a life worthwhile" Albert Einstein.* **24**

6. *"Act alone and you will have tried. Act together and you will achieve"* **28**

7. *"Open a book and feed your mind."* **31**

8. *"Be bold, Be brave, Be inspired."* **34**

9. *"Embrace the unknown, that's the mystery of your gift"* **38**

10. *"You deserve to be loved"* **42**

11. *" Spread love everywhere you go, let no one ever come to you without leaving happier." Mother Teresa.* **44**

12. *"Fortune favours the bold."* **47**

13. *"If you believe in luck, be lucky."* **50**

14. *"Keep your face to the sunshine, you cannot see the shadows."* **55**

Granny Lane Again

CHAPTERS

1 *"Nothing ventured, nothing gained."* **59**

2. *"The courage you need comes from you."* **62**

3. *"Always remember that you are unique, just like everyone else," Margaret Mead.* **67**

4. *"Do foolish things but do them with enthusiasm."* **71**

5. *"Hold your nerve, the storm will pass."* **74**

Granny Lane's World Collapses

CHAPTERS

1. *"A bit of a struggle is good for the soul."* 80

2. *"Love is like a vine, if you don't tend it you will lose it."* 86

3. *"Don't float through life, make some waves."* 98

4. *"If you want rainbows, then please accept the rain."* 102

5. *"Whoever is happy will make others happy too." Anne Frank.* 108

Dedication:

Thanks to Christian who gave me the creative idea and the people who believed in me and gave me their support and encouragement.

You know who you are.

You are my Angels.

Granny Lane's Christmas

CHAPTER 1

"Life is not a rehearsal, live it."

Louise was lonely. She knew Christmas Day in her new home of one month would be a quiet day, a lonely day even. Looking back over the year she reflected on how busy it had been. Retired and suddenly widowed she had moved eight miles from the city to the suburbs. The idea had come from her children and she had strongly refused at first but after a great deal of heart searching, she had come to the same decision, that, in fact, it was a good idea.

Luke, her son, tall, erect and blond haired like his father, had followed in his footsteps and joined the Army. As he was still on tour and not due home until February he would be unable to visit at Christmas with Maria, his wife and Honey and Sam her grandchildren. Her daughter, Amy, who had chosen her career when only 10 years old on their first package holiday to Portugal was an Air Steward, scheduled to travel to Singapore, her dream destination, so she wouldn't see her either.

Well prepared she had planned a day of treats. First, breakfast in bed. Croissants had been her first choice but the thought of buttery crumbs on her best bedding deterred her. Then there was boiled egg but once again the idea of waiting for an egg to boil the exact time that she liked them and then fiddling with cracking open an egg on a wobbly surface foiled her plan. Finally she had chosen simple and delicious wholemeal toast, butter and Whisky Marmalade [bought at a Summer Fair], Lemon and Ginger Tea and a new book. The idea, as ideas do, seemed foolproof but the mixture of old bones and an active personality didn't agree.

Moving house had been a shock at first. Downsizing they had called it in the Estate Agent's Office which makes it sound like an easy and neat package but UPROOTING was more apt. She had to admit though that selling her house, moving into another one, choosing what to keep and what to pass on to another life had kept her busy and sometimes she had no time to linger on the sadness that had engulfed her life. Even now the little bedroom was stacked with unopened boxes which had already spent long years in garages and attics containing items which had at one time belonged to either her parents or those of her husband Jeff, not forgetting their own stored memories.

So, still dressed in her nightie and dressing-gown belted tightly around her tiny form, she decided to unpack some more of her boxes of books into the empty bookcases waiting in the lounge. Later, happy that another job had been done she showered and put on her new festive pyjamas, dressing-gown and slippers, all presents from her loving family, and let her favourite chair wrap it's bulky arms around her.

Switching on the television, which she knew would be guaranteed to bring her pleasure, she let out a little sigh. Gazing out of the little window at the trees in the distance, leafless now, she felt the promise of Spring and a new future for her.

CHAPTER 2

"Believe you can and you're halfway there." Theodore Roosevelt.

New Year's Day arrived. This new year with a change of home meant a new life and she needed a resolution. Not that Louise ever resorted to those silly notions. Such things, she considered, were to be left to the young. Resolutions like going on a diet and joining a gym or giving up smoking or alcohol rarely lasted a month in her opinion. Anyway for her, it was not a resolution she needed as being busy had been a lifesaver for her.

A new plaque on the wall in the hall, a gift from her daughter picked up on one of her travels said, 'Life is not a rehearsal. Live it.' She reached up and touched it every day. It gave her resolve.

It was Aisha, who, with her husband Ali, ran the grocery store in the High Street, who changed her destiny.

'Good morning Mrs. R. How are you? You look a little pale today,' chirped Aisha, as she entered the welcoming shop.

'I'm fine, just feeling a little lost and lonely today.'

'We can't have that. You need to join a group or club or even become a volunteer. My mother is always out somewhere with her friends. She keeps on telling us to produce some grandchildren to keep her busy. Why don't we look at the cards on the advertisement board in the window. Here, come and see.'

Following Aisha's slender sari-wrapped frame to the front of the shop they were soon scanning the large wooden board speckled with notices ranging from trader's advertisements, language tutors and music teachers to items for private sale.

'Ah yes, here's the one I was thinking of. There's a Knit and Natter group every Monday afternoon in a room at the back of the Coffee Shop. I know it. It's just off the High Street behind the trendy Art Shop. And Monday, that's today. Why don't you go. It starts at two. Several of the ladies come in for their weekly magazines and they seem such a cheerful lot.'

'But I can't knit,' grinned Louise her spirits rising.'

'I'm sure they must need someone to sew things together and someone will teach you to knit or crochet squares to make blankets. I've seen one in a raffle and they are gorgeous,' was the encouraging answer.

Aisha was right. Her first job was to unravel a whole carrier bag of tangled wool whilst listening to the gossip and groans covering everything from the latest T.V. drama to sorting out world problems and watching busy hands knitting tiny hats and clothes for premature babies in the city hospital or lap-blankets for the old people in the retirement home a few miles away. It was like a production line.

This was just the project she needed, something she could get her teeth into, metaphorically so to speak. After fighting the monstrous muddle of multicoloured threads that could have come from Joseph's technicoloured dreamcoat a tiny hat for a premature baby she thought would be a snitch. That is after she had conquered the abbreviated language: k=knit, p=purl, k2tog=knit two stitches together, psso=pass slip stitch over. Even this task was further complicated by the fact that there different ways to cast on, e.g. using two needles or by the thumb method and if you choose the former method, then knitting in the front of the stitch or between stitches. Advice and friendship came from all around the room. Maeve, an advanced knitter, who would often come and sit next to her could knit a baby's hat in less than an hour but with Louise's stiff fingers and inexperience her first effort took one week and no amount of gently pressing with the tip of a warm iron and stretching could erase her hat's unusual shape but to her it was beautiful.

Pauline, the glamourous red-head of the group, insisted that crochet work grew quicker so Louise was put to master the intricacies of another language, e.g. ch=chain, dc=double crochet and htr=half treble and given a pattern for a baby's jacket using only the three stitches of that strange language hoping that one day it could be worn by the first of Aisha and Ali's family.

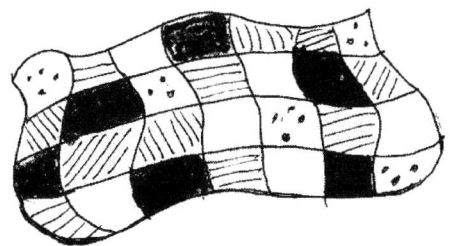

CHAPTER 3
"A book is like a garden in your pocket"
Chinese Proverb

After a short while Louise's life was changed once again by a benevolent hand.

'Listen up everyone', a raised voice held everyone's attention. 'Pat, the manager of the charity shop rang me this morning with the news that a big bag of knitting wool has been handed in and she is holding it back for us to have first choice. So put your hands in your purses girls and get there sooner than later.'

The speaker was Brenda, whom she had found lived near her, not the Brenda who energetically walked the mile and a half from her house and back to get, as she called it, her 6000 steps a day.

(Putting a tag to names was her way of remembering them!) Later Brenda's voice from over her shoulder whispered, 'The charity shop is up by the church, next to the Pilgrims' Rest Pub. The knitting's coming on by the way. Good work.'

When, the next day, they bumped into each other, (not literally of course) in Aisha and Ali's store, Brenda said, 'Have you found our charity shop yet? I volunteer there every Tuesday afternoon.

I am on my way there now. Why don't we walk there together?'

Louise wasn't surprised that she was soon persuaded to be a volunteer. She found herself enjoying watching people buy once loved items which needed a new home.

In fact sometimes watching and secretly smiling as some of her own donations of china and books found another loving home. She loved especially, encouraging children to spend their pocket-money pennies on books and persuaded Pat to create a children' area where they could sit and look at and read books, thus allowing their mum or dad or even grandparent the opportunity to pick up a bargain elsewhere in the shop. 'That's called good marketing,' said Pat. 'We need more people like you and many hands make light work too.'

Growing up as an only child books had become a passion, some of which had been stored in the garage of her old home.

They smelt musty with age and one, a dark maroon covered encyclopaedia with a mouse nibbled corner, now rested on a table in the corner of the lounge waiting to be opened. She was almost afraid of the childhood memories it would reveal.

One day a lady of a similar age to herself came into the shop and shyly asked if these was any chance that a golf set might be in the back room. Checking, Louise came back empty handed, saying, 'No, I'm afraid not but if you keep coming in I'm sure we'll get one.'

She was thinking of her husband's golf set now standing in the corner of the over-burdened little bedroom not being used. It had been a retirement gift from colleagues and friends and had given many hours of pleasure, exercise and friendship.

So the next time her special customer came into the shop she was able to greet her with raised eyebrows, a nod and a smile and any regret or sadness was dispelled when she was rewarded by enthusiastic thanks. 'How wonderful. It will give my husband such pleasure. He is finding retirement difficult and..... (she grinned) it will get him from under my feet too.'

As she watched the shiny golf clubs in their smart navy wrap disappear out of the shop she realised that there was no use in hoarding when they could live a happy life with someone else.

The woman had reminded her of herself and Jeff when they had taken the unsteady steps into retirement and she had nipped into the back of the shop, leaving Pat to serve , whilst she wiped away a few poignant tears.

CHAPTER 4
"Love, Laugh and Live."

Downsizing, disastrous as it had once felt didn't completely stop the routine that Louise and Jeff had created for themselves in retirement. Only dropping away from the U.3.A. (University of the Third Age) meetings with their monthly speakers on a Thursday and the off-shoot of Art for Pleasure because she missed his company, she had continued to keep Fridays for a trip to the city. Friday had always been a window-shopping day finishing with an early evening meal in a restaurant overlooking the river.

Still journeying to the city, now by local transport, Friday had become Market Day and a treat of afternoon tea in a little cafe overlooking the ancient cobbled Market Square. Once a thriving Ice Cream Parlour in the 1960's it had been expanded into a cosy cafe serving the traders, regulars and visitors.

After a busy shopping spree, always buying much more than she could comfortably manage, she looked forward to parking her pull-along shopper beside her in her favourite window seat (if free) and watching the people milling among the heavily laden market stalls.

As she shouldered open the heavy toughened glass door, burdened by her heavy load , the old fashioned exterior gave way to a bright candy coloured interior and the heady mixture of sugar and vanilla from the ice-cream bar and the intoxicating aromas from the Italian coffee machine in the cafe.

'Buon giorno Fifi', boomed a heavily accented voice across the room. 'I have your special table ready for you.'

Blushing she replied, 'Buon giorno Giovanni', and quickly slipped into the offered seat.

Giovanni, the dark, wavy-haired manager, always teasingly called her Fifi, short for favourite Friday friend and always fussed around her giving her extra clotted cream for her scone or extra delicious home-made strawberry jam for her toasted teacake. He sometimes shared banter with Mad Max as he called the young leather-clad motor cyclist who came in for his regular banana milk shake and showered the little pretty golden haired teenager, who came in for hot chocolate for her stall-holder boss and a can of fizzy juice for herself with Italian love songs.

With the background hum of happy customers and occasional aromas from the kitchen she would sit back and reflect that life was good. She had learnt to knit and crochet and she could manage the excentricities of the cash machine at the charity shop when Pat was in the back room and she had made some lovely new friends. And accepting that missing her life companion was natural she let herself be charmed by a gentleman such as Giovanni, once in a while.

CHAPTER 5
"Only a life lived for others is a life worthwhile" Albert Einstein.

It wasn't Aisha or Brenda who suggested the next turning point in her life but Pat.

'You love meeting people so why don't you volunteer at the big hall at the other side of town, you know, the National Trust one. The number 39 bus passes right near it.'

' Why hadn't I thought of that,' said Louise, 'My husband and I spent many happy hours exploring stately homes and gardens. I often wondered what it would be like to become one of the people who try to keep historic places alive. Thanks Pat, I'll do something about it.'

Within no time it seemed the history of the hall seeped into her veins and sometimes, when a budding historian or antique buff asked a question of her that was a little beyond her knowledge, she would take herself off to the city library to once again bury herself in books.

Being a volunteer didn't stop her from pretending to be a visitor too. One sunny afternoon, on her way to the exit to catch her bus, passing the entrance to the high, red-bricked walled Victorian garden she noticed a new sign which appealed to her sense of humour saying 'Bookworms welcome here.' It was a notice no avid book lover could resist. Laid out in strict rectangular plots the garden was an engaging treasure box of colour with fruit and flowers, trees and herbs in profusion and in the far corner, opposite the newly painted and restored greenhouse was a new summer house with white lace curtained windows to tempt the curious reader in.

Finding a book to add to her already bulging bookcase was easy but as she stepped out the sharp sunlight pierced her eyes. A sun-beaten hand grabbed her elbow and a deep, warm voice at her side said, 'Take care, Lass. Ground's a bit damp after yesterday's storm.'

Looking up, the brown hands changed to an even more tanned face topped with a mass of thick grey curls and the most vivid green eyes. That was when she met Pete, a retired seaman, who like her was a volunteer and attached to the gardens.

'Oh, thank you,' she gratefully replied with a smile. 'The sun was in my eyes. Isn't the garden beautiful?'

'Thanks, I help here. My name's Pete by the way. Do you have a garden?'

' Oh, yes, yes I do. A new garden. Well not new. I've moved house and I am changing the garden.' And with that, encouraged by the friendly rugged smiles she went on to explain how she had set out to change her garden from an overgrown patch of Azaleas, Laurels and weeds to a haven of herbs, fruit and vegetables and of how her family and friends had filled it in no time with an apple, a cherry and a plum tree as well as aromatic rosemary, lavender and thyme.

'I've got an allotment. I'll have to see what I can give you.' And so a new relationship blossomed.

Louise's house was the last house in the road, at the other end from the church and her back garden was bordered by a lane called Sandpit Lane which was a public footpath.

Walkers with hiking boots and haversacks, dog owners with all range of dogs from Dachshunds to Dalmatians, and excited children in brightly coloured wellington boots would often pass her gate.

They were frequently greeted by a cheerful smile and a pleasant greeting from a slight, scruffily dressed figure with a silver-grey bob and sparkling blue eyes. She knew where they were going as she had taken to walking that way herself.

The lane soon led through rolling countryside to a wooded valley where a pretty cascading river raced to the sea.

CHAPTER 6
"Act alone and you will have tried. Act together and you will achieve"

Life changed for that sole occupant of the house next to the lane when two children came to live next door with their father. At first they seemed very wary of her and rarely lifted their downcast faces when she occasionally passed them. One day there was a tentative tap on the front door and there stood a little girl framed in the vast void, her little brother standing scuffing his heels in the gravel at the beginning of the lane.

'Daddy's not home. He's always there to meet us off the school bus. We don't know what to do,' said the shivering girl softly.

On hearing the girl's heartfelt plea Louise quickly told them that she would put a note on their door so that their daddy would know where they were. 'You can come and have a drink of milk and biscuits in my kitchen while you wait. Would you like to do that?'

She suppressed a smile hoping her words 'a glass of milk and a biscuit' didn't make her sound like the wicked witch of the Hansel and Gretal fairytale. Soon after, making sure they had no allergies like her granddaughter had, they were sat at the kitchen table drinking and eating and drawing pictures on her best writing vellum (she was an avid writers of letters) with black lead pencils and ball-point pens. When the doorbell rang they leapt up shouting, 'Daddy, that'll be Daddy.'

Louise looked up into the worried soft grey eyes of the tall man with an unruly shock of hair just like his son's filling the doorframe. 'Hello, you must be Daddy. As you can see they are safe and sound,' and she turned to nod to the children who were gathering up their coats and satchels.

'Come in and have a cuppa whilst they finish their milk and biscuits. You look cold yourself.'

Comfortably installed, wrapping his hands around the welcome mug of hot chocolate he thanked her and explained why he was late and that he was on his own as their mother had died of 'the big C'.

'Our Mummy's dead. She could speak French you know. She came from a place called Brittany. It's like the word Britain but it's not Britain. It's not far away. We go there every holiday to see our grand'mère and grand'père. I am learning French at school,' explained the now talkative girl.

'I can't remember my Mummy but I can say the days of the week and count up to one hundred.

She's called Oceane and I'm Louis. Grand-père calls us his three Muskateers. She's Athos, I'm Aramis and Daddy is Porthos.' chatted the little boy now finding his feet.

'Sorry, they can really chatter. My name, by the way, is Dan, short for Daniel.'

'That's O.K. My name is Mrs. Ry.....'

'We know, it's Granny Lane,' interrupted the excited duo.

In silence the two adults' eyes met and Dan, raising his eyebrows and smiling said, 'Children will be children. Hello Granny Lane.'

CHAPTER 7
"Open a book and feed your mind."

That first summer floated into the mellow mists of Autumn. The children soon became regular visitors (with their father's consent, of course) sometimes doing their homework in the cosy kitchen. Working in a charity shop she had started to buy beautiful used children's books for her charges and they soon became bookworms like herself. She had always loved books, they had been her teachers, friends and comforters.

The children were naturally curious and she answered their questions as simply as she could despite her years, trying to see the world as they saw it. One day when they were seated in the little lounge in front of the log fire Louis said, 'What's in the red box on the table in the corner?' Bewildered she turned to look at the object he had referred to and realised he had noticed the aged, embossed, blood-red cover of a childhood encyclopaedia, worn with its journey through time. It was no longer hidden in boxes, moved from one cold attic to another decade after decade and nibbled by mice in a garage . In the dark corner it lay, almost out of sight, teasing her to open it in a forboding way, taunting her. She had been 12 years of age when it had come into her life just before a sad time. She still wasn't ready to open 'Pandora's Box' as she called it, afraid of the memories it might unlock.

' It's not a box. It's an encyclopaedia, a book with lots of interesting information in it. I was given it for Christmas when I was a little girl and it became very precious. I haven't had time to open it yet.'

Just then the doorbell rang and the children ran to the door shouting , 'That'll be Daddy,' and the moment thankfully passed. She reflected that she was not ready to open it and wondered if she ever would. She had loved it. Given to her before her grandparents sadly died she had retreated into its contents.

The run up to Christmas became a busy time with Christmas cards to send some with letters which, this year, would contain happier news of her new life.

The Knit and Natter group had been making ornaments and little gifts to be sold at the church's Christmas Fair and at the charity shop the volunteers had put aside Christmassy items for Imogen, who came down from London to visit her parents, to work her magic in the window.

The Old Hall, opening for a week, was decorated

with holly and ivy gathered by Pete and his army of volunteers.

Christmas Day passed, not lonely this year, but with Luke, Marie, Holly and Sam and later in the week with Amy and her partner Rachael walking in the nearby countryside and dining at the Pilgrims' Rest. All was right with the world.

CHAPTER 8
"Be bold, Be brave, Be inspired."

'The second year is usually the worst'.
The comment came when she wasn't feeling at her best, it being mid February when most people got the 'winter blues'. The remark wasn't aimed at her but she had heard it and it hurt. It struck a nerve and gave her cause to think about her life. Yes, she accepted that she missed Jeff but she had moved on and moving on meant meeting people in the same situation whether retired, widowed, divorced, separated or just single, all essentially lonely. In her case after 50 years of marriage, a career and bringing up two children it would be a natural state at first but in the past year her life had taken a turn for the best. Louise's skills at the Knit and Natter had improved and she had mastered the idiosyncracies of the cash machine at the charity shop which had been alien to her. She had persuaded, Susan, who had bought Jeff's golf-clubs , to become a volunteer and she had brought a friend with her.

The air was crisp and fresh on an early Spring day and as Louise walked up the High Street the sun turned its rays on the window of the charity shop it was obvious that Imogen, once again, had worked her magic. A mannequin, dressed in a daffodil yellow suit fit for a wedding with hat, gloves, shoes and handbag to complement, overshadowed a little white, metal garden table holding two jugs containing 'pretend' fruit juice and lemon slices and an array of glasses. It was so eye-catching that it led to Louise's next project. (Would she never learn!)

It was a few days later that fate stepped in. A skip arrived outside a house near the church and began to be filled with building rubble and unwanted contents from the house and garden. No stranger to the contents of skips, as her newly designed garden paths were edged with broken terracotta bricks from several of those treasure chests, she kept a daily eye on its contents. It wasn't long before an old blue folding camping table appeared.

'It's a bit old love,' said the friendly builder who she had come to know as Mitch, 'One leg looks a bit wonky.'

'I'll fix it somehow. It's just the job. Many thanks.'

'No need for you to carry it. I'll drop it off after work on my way home. The house by the lane did you say?'

With a scrub and a splint made from an old wooden spoon and black electrical tape she found in her husband's toolbox the table began its new life. From then on, each weekend, it stood by the side of the gate in the lane for the weary and footsore walkers ending their walks to restore their energy. The table held a variety of glasses (from the charity shop of course) and an 'honesty box'. Underneath in large jugs, their feet keeping cool in an old washing-up bowl full of cold water, stood home-made lemonade. Two bowls for their doggie friends were laid close by.

In no time at all there were people to talk to and dogs to stroke and requests for the recipe for the delicious lemonade which, she explained, had been her Mother's. It wasn't long before copies were printed by Aisha and Ali and inserted in a tin under the table with a request for donations to be put in the 'honesty box'.

Traditional Still Lemonade

Serves 8 – 10 Ready in 20 minutes plus cooling and chilling.

3 unwaxed lemons + 1 more for serving.

150 gr. Caster Sugar.

Halve and squeeze the 3 lemons, reserving the peel. Put the peel in a pan with the sugar and 500 ml. Water. Bring to a simmer and heat until the sugar dissolves. Set aside until cool.

Squeeze any liquid from the peel into the pan, then discard. Pour the sugar into a measuring jug through a sieve and stir in the reserved lemon juice. Top up to 1 litre with cold water. Transfer to a jug or a bottle and chill.

CHAPTER 9

"Embrace the unknown, that's the mystery of your gift"

During the summer months Louisa's life began to slip into a dangerously comfortable pattern. The trouble was she liked challenges and 'projects' as she called them, which often involved research (usually in the library), learning something new (at the Knit and Natter group) and gardening. They kept her busy and she was able to have conversations with the people she met.

She now thought of herself as the 'The Granny down the lane' and she found out, after questioning a few friends, that it had originated from the times when she was working in the garden and her habit of smiling and saying hello to passers-by.

She didn't always work at the charity shop now that Susan and her friend Betty could hold the fort but never missed going to the Hall. Pete always looked out for her and they often had their packed lunches together, he with his cheese and pickle sandwiches and she with a box of salad and a piece of fruit. From their bench in the old orchard they enjoyed watching the trees turn from apple blossom to Autumn bounty whilst chatting about their respective families. She learnt that 'his beautiful Mary' had recently died and he spent a lot of time in his allotment when not at the Hall. She quietly noticed how his eyes misted with pride when he talked of his son who ran in marathons for the local hospice in his mother's memory.

It was because of her time at the Hall that she met Molly, the pretty, shy, auburn-haired helper at the Central Library on her occasional Friday visits. Researching for information on the Green Man Molly had led her on her slow journey into the use of a computer and in return she would buy her a hot chocolate and tell her about the countryside that opened up at the bottom of Sandpit Lane.

'You must always knock and see me if you are passing. Mind you, always check the back garden first as that's where I'll probably be.'

'I will, I'd love to see your garden too,' said Molly enthusiastically.

So, from Fridays to Wednesdays she found herself pleasantly occupied.

Reluctant at first, to stay at home and return to feeling lonely, Granny Lane had begun to like Thursdays because she could have conversations with two callers at the house. She had met Steve, the regular postman, shortly after moving in when she had to thank him for leaving her keys, inadvertently left in the front door lock, with a neighbour. Then there was the day she had left a carrier-bag of groceries on the doorstep. She had answered the doorbell to a tall, curly-haired young man who assured her that people who had just moved, young or old sometimes struggled with their new routine. Over a period of time, she heard of his good deeds; checking when curtains are undrawn or milk bottles are not taken in. Once he had been accosted by a screaming old lady in her nightdress who forced him to have a look at her husband. He had promptly called an ambulance.

'Did you always want to be a postman, Steve?'

'Yes, It was me dad really, who started it. He went to sea but when he met me mam he was besotted with her and he sent picture postcards from all the ports around the world that they called at declaring his love. If he had no shore leave he'd get a mate to send one with just an 'X'. We knew the code. I loved those cards and their fascinating stamps. He has them in a box on the dresser to see all the time now that me mam's gone.'

'Oh, what a lovely story. Thanks for telling me.'

Then there was the window-cleaner, a young man from Poland who talked longingly of his wife and two little girls back home and of how he was hoping to save enough to build a business and bring them over to England to be together again.

How she loved the energy and enthusiasm of young people!

CHAPTER 10
"You deserve to be loved"

'You like me to take that old table to the rubbish place?' enquired Jacob, the window cleaner when he eyed the old weary-looking table Louisa had cleaned the day before, ready for it's weekend mission. 'Oh, no, no, no, that has a precious job to do at the weekend. It still has life in it,' telling him proudly of her weekend task.

On another occasion he said, 'Your garden is nice. I see gardens not like this. It has plants very different. You have one. It is a plant that grows everywhere at home in Poland. Lena my wife.

We go and see her mother. She makes it. My two girls, Zofia and Hanna call it her special soup. Sometimes it is called Hungarian Sorrel Soup but we call it Polish Sorrel Soup.' Her garden was now redesigned and full to the brim with plants often given to her by family and friends. Sorrel, given to her by a special friend, Sue from University days, led her back to the library once more.

This tiny cutting had established itself rapidly and she was curious as how to add it to her ever expanding collection of healthy recipes. This time she was shown, by a charming young man, how to negotiate the computer and take a photocopy. The now proud possesser of the recipe for Polish Sorrel Soup the tangy result was made throughout the summer and frozen for the winter.

There were times when Granny Lane doubted her own actions though. Take the day she had gone on a Gardening Club outing and returned home to find the table surrounded by a small group of puzzled walkers and their dogs discussing the curious scene before them. Standing in one of the doggie bowls stood an empty bottle of gin, topped with a battered old brown hat and on the table lay a smashed honesty box.

After a short while a happy intoxicated tramp was found in her summer house amongst the cushions and blankets stored there who ended his day sleeping in the local police station. Meanwhile the bemused crowd were content with a fresh glass of commercial fruit juice and wended their way home with exciting tales to tell at work and at school on Monday morning.

CHAPTER 11

" Spread love everywhere you go, let no one ever come to you without leaving happier." Mother Teresa.

A wet summer ran into a misty Autumn, neighbours had become friends, and strangers in the lane had lingered long enough to become short term acquaintances too. Life was good.

Winter came early and suddenly wind came from the north and east but walkers still walked and Louise pondered over how to provide her weary winter wanderers with a warming treat.

The answer came from the charity shop once again. Someone had kindly donated two thermos flasks so now her weekly trips to the farmers market in town would provide her with fresh carrots from the farms north of the city.

A miscellany of mugs (from guess where) were soon filled with hot Spicy Carrot and Lentil Soup, a family favourite, taken from a student cookbook of her university days, were warming empty stomachs and chilled hands.

She had taken to sitting in the back bedroom window which gave her a view of the lane and it seemed to her that, beside the gate , people were lingering longer to make friends instead of moving on. News filtered back to her that it was there, under her holly tree laden with crimson berries, that Thomas the butcher's apprentice had met his sweetheart Molly. The nervous apprentice had, at first, always stammered his answer to her cheerful greetings but, in time, his confidence grew and her greetings often led to deeper conversations accompanied by a cautious grin. She wasn't surprised that Molly, her Molly from the library, had been just his match. It was there, too, that eleven year old Simon had found a new husband for his Mum and a great step-dad for himself.

News spreads. A locally born chef from a 'posh' hotel in the countryside, a keen walker himself and with a Polish window-cleaner, had heard of her profusion of Sorrel and occasionally came for supplies to make a special sauce. Fame comes from unusual quarters!

Before long a new recipe was stored in the tin under the table, surplus herbs and potted cuttings too were added. The honesty box grew heavier each day.

Spicy Carrot and Lentil Soup

Ingredients:

2 medium onions, finely chopped.

1 tablespoon vegetable oil.

4 large carrots, scrubbed and chopped.

200 g. Red lentils.

2 level teaspoons of mild curry powder. (Add more if needed)

1 litre of stock, (chicken or vegetable). Add more if needed.

Method:

Heat the oil and fry the onions over a low heat for about 5 minutes, add the carrots and cook for a further 3 minutes. Stir in the curry powder and cook for one minute stirring well. Add stock and lentils. Bring to the boil and simmer gently for 30 minutes or until the carrots and lentils are soft. Liquidise and add more water if needed.

CHAPTER 12
"Fortune favours the bold."

'We need a theme for Christmas at the church,' announced Maureen, putting down her knitting. It was a balmy October day and Christmas was far from the minds of the occupants of the little back room at the coffee shop behind the High Street.

'Christmas. What do you mean by a theme? You have the Nativity and the Three Kings don't you?' asked Eileen, the curious newcomer to the group.

'Well, we always do the Nativity, of course. We've done it in so many different ways; with a real donkey, with all the Sunday School children dressed up in something, we've even done audience participation. You name it, we've tried it and now we are looking for something else.'

Despite an afternoon of discussion nobody came up with an idea.

The church had, in Louise's childhood, filled her life, but moving on through university, work and marriage she had drifted away. It was easy to be pulled back. Maureen and two other ladies in the Knit and Natter group were in the W.I. and met one evening in the vestry. There were some young people too and the opportunity to meet the younger generation appealed to her as she felt young at heart herself.

Friday was still 'a visit to the city day' but she had taken to leaving the house earlier in order to visit second-hand furniture shops as well as charity shops for a replacement for the table in the lane. The trusty table was, by now, becoming a little unsteady (like her she thought) and needed replacing. As she was now captivated by the idea of finding a Christmas theme she had added it to her search too. Always ending her day at Giovanni's cafe this Friday was no exception but there was no booming greeting, instead his son was behind the counter.

'Hello Mateo, Nice to see you again. Helping your Dad out are you at this busy time of year?'

'Helping out, yes but not as you say. We are still short staffed as Dad's had a fall in the back yard by the bins. He's not too bad, broken his arm in two places and is in for observation. He's made friends with the guy in the next bed whose son is a postman. You should hear the tales they tell. To be truthful he is being spoilt by two WRVS volunteers called Bernadette and Marie who come round with a trolley of treats, magazines and the such like and they enjoy his teasing banter. You know what he's like!'

She smiled and nodded her head, 'And the nurses too, probably.' At that point Mateo was called away to the kitchen.

Finishing her coffee she left, only to return a while later with a box of chocolates, a huge 'Get Well' card signed by all the market traders and a basket of fruit from the fruit and vegetable stall persuading all the customers in the cafe to sign it too. The cosy cafe was not the same place without Giovanni.

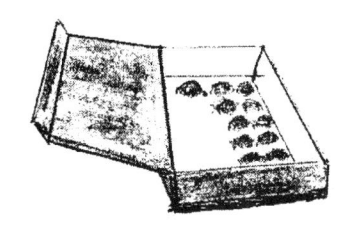

CHAPTER 13
"If you believe in luck, be lucky."

The angel appeared in the Curiosity Shop next to the cathedral. It didn't really 'appear', it fell out of a book as she picked it off the shelf. The book, on origami, she had considered might be handy when Oceane and Louis spent time with her. The article, for that was what it was, showed how to make a sculptured angel out of stiff white card or cardboard. Ideal for mature hands but no good for the children, nevertheless intrigued by the book and the article she had bought it.

The idea of angels, however, flew around her mind for a couple of days but by Monday afternoon she could contain her enthusiasm no longer.

'I've found it, I've found it. An angel fell out of a book. I've found the Nativity project for the church. You could make them from all kinds, wool, paper, wood. We could knit, crochet, sew. Oh, all kinds of things.'

' Slow down, slow down. An angel fell on you did we hear you say,' interrupted Brenda her friend from down the street.

'Well, not literally. Look here,' and she produced a perfect sculpted figure in pure white, blowing a trumpet. 'This is only an idea, we could knit, the W.I. could sew, the Sunday School children could draw.' The words tumbled out like a raging river.

'I've got a knitted angel pattern ,' pitched in Brenda.

'And I've got a fabric one,' said Maureen. 'Wait until I tell the W.I. about this. They'll be thrilled.'

'The younger children can draw their own pictures or colour in and the older ones can make those folded paper ones,' said someone in the corner.

Maxine, the wife of the baker in the High Street added, 'We can make fairy cakes only call them angel cakes and tip the wings with edible gold and have them after the service.'

' What a brilliant idea. I wonder if you can get angel-shaped biscuit cutters? I'll have a look on line,' said Pattie, an enthusiastic cook.

The ideas poured in but Elaine, our newcomer, said, 'What about me. I can't knit yet.'

Reminded of her first tentative steps to join the group Louise said, 'No problem, you can make pom-pom snowballs using a pom-pom maker. It's dead easy. Not like the old days when you had to cut rounds out of cornflake packets and wind the wool round and round. Just this week we've been given a bag of white wool so we have plenty to start with.'

As time passed angels filled the church. Knitted angels, crocheted angels, drawings made by the little children and strings of paper angels by the willing teenagers, rag-doll angels and an angel made of wood by the men's group.

At the beginning of December there appeared by the welcoming wooden porch a metal angel made by Bert, the scrap dealer. It stood so tall that it could be seen all the way down the High Street by both pedestrians and vehicles and was considered a danger at night, by some, when car lights shone on it. Many a passer-by would stand and gaze at it trying to find a utensil or pan handle that had once been theirs. Angelic forms fluttered down the street and could be found in the windows of shops and homes as the Christmas theme. Visitors flocked to the High Street and spent their money. Shops and restaurants and cafes flourished and the Pilgrims' Rest was always packed full at lunchtimes.

On Christmas Day the church was filled to overflowing . There were angels everywhere to celebrate the magic of the birth of a baby born in a stable.

KNITTED CHRISTMAS ANGEL

Small amounts of DK yarn. Size 8/4mm. Needles. Large eyed needle. Small amount of Stuffing.

BODY: Cast on 48 stitches.

Row 1: Knit.

Row 2: Purl

Row 3: *K2tog, K 10, repeat until end of row. [44 sts]

Row 4: Purl

Row 5: Knit

Row 6: P2tog, P9, repeat until end of row. * [40 sts]

Continue as given from * to * decreasing on every third row until Row 20 has been worked.

Row 21: K2tog, K4, repeat until end of row. [20 sts]

Row 22: Starting with a purl row continue in stocking stitch until Row 34 has been worked.

[Note: Row 27: Insert a marker to show neck.]

Row 35: K2tog. to end.

Row 36: Purl.

Row 37: Knit.

Row 38: P2tog to end.

Leaving a length of yarn long enough to sew up, thread the yarn through the stitches and tighten to make the top of head. Turn the angel inside out and sew up head and body. At the marker run some stitches around and draw up lightly. Stuff the head, tighten thread to mark neck.

WINGS: Cast on 27 sts.

Row 1: Knit.

Row 2: Knit.

Row 3: Knit decreasing at each end.

Knit a further 11 rows decreasing at each end. Cast off. Join wings to back of angel.

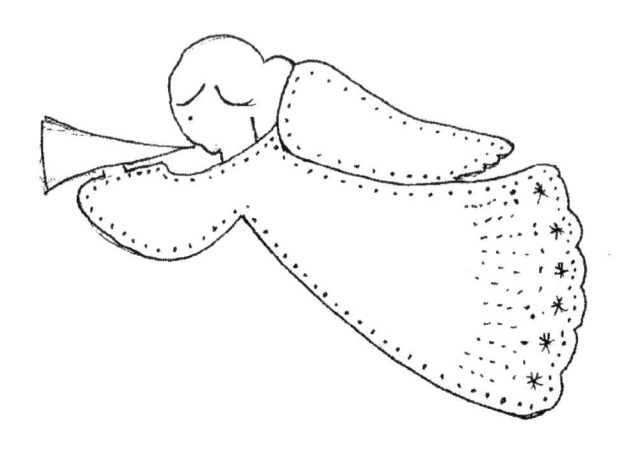

CHAPTER 14

"Keep your face to the sunshine, you cannot see the shadows."

Boxing Day greeted her with sharp sunlight squeezing through a gap in her curtains. She snuggled into her new festive dressing gown covered with snowflakes, bought on one of her daughter's trips to Scandinavia. Smiling to herself she felt that today was going to be another good day. Her precious family would be coming, and they would walk in the countryside that began in 'her lane'.

She knew that there would be walkers passing her door, some new, and some familiar faces amongst them, all keen to exercise their over-filled stomachs and to fill their lungs with fresh country air, children with their new warming winter wear and dogs of all sizes with their smart winter coats and shiny new collars.

Holly and Sam, now teenagers reluctant at first to be separated from their new technology, helped her to fill the two flasks with ruby-red soup, made from tomatoes and red peppers, to give a festive feel to the day and Luke and Marie picked sprays of red-berried holly from a tree in the lane to add to the theme. Knowing of his mother's 'project' he had brought a box of shortbread biscuits to add to the treats.

As they walked down the lane further she reflected on how much she loved the little tree-embraced lane that must have known countless tramping feet through the ages, leafless now with the sun, now weakened by an encroaching winter mist, reaching through the woven wooden canopy.

In the distance, the racing river that endlessly forged its way to the sea could be heard. Today it was high, too high she noticed when they reached it. Too high she thought and she felt concern for the houses downstream that might lay in its pathway.

On the way back they could hear sounds of laughter and as they rounded the corner saw a crowd. From their response it was apparent that they were waiting for her and, in place of her faithful old table stood a new stainless steel stand piled high with little packages and envelopes, all for her.

There, stood Giovanni, his arm in a sling, standing next to his new friend Pete, who now carried a stick. Steve was there, too, holding Pete's arm. (of course, why hadn't she seen the resemblance!) There was Brenda, her first friend and dear neighbour, Thomas and Molly with arms wrapped around each other and walkers she recognised with their doggie friends. Too many to list here.

The little house rang with laughter and love that afternoon and when all her visitors had gone Granny Lane sat in her favourite chair, feeling it cradling her weary body. 'What a wonderful Christmas it has been,' she told herself. She reached for the familiar maroon-backed book. She could open it now. The book knew only one thing, that once opened the knowledge and memories it contained would be like jewels in a crown.

Granny Lane looked around and remembered that first lonely Christmas and felt loved and contented.

Granny Lane Again

CHAPTER 1
"Nothing ventured, nothing gained."

Having successfully manoeuvred the last two years since downsizing, with more good luck than management, Louise started the New Year with her usual cheerful optimism.

Remembering her mother's words of warning, 'Christmas decorations must be removed by 12th night or else bad luck will come' she decided to pack away early. There were only a few as she had given their artificial tree, which was of a good age, and all the lights and decorations, to the local Scout Group for their hut and most of what she had now were angels of course.

Whilst leaving her Christmas cards, ready to go in the charity collection bin at the local supermarket, on the kitchen table, the festive cake tin caught her eye, and she was tempted by the last mince pie from the local bakery which had been decorated with angel wings designed by enthusiastic Maxine.

What a Christmas it had been. As a result of her vision there had been angels everywhere, at the church of course, down the High Street, up the side roads and in the surrounding homes.

They were all around her too, in the form of family, friends and neighbours.

The next day the sign 'House for Sale' on the house opposite changed to 'Sold' and a skip arrived which was like a red rag to a bull, (which is a fallacy by the way). Then the builders arrived. At first nothing overly exciting happened as far as she could see. (Not that she is nosey you understand. Anyway she was rarely at home.) It was the contents of the skip that intrigued her. At first there was only builders' rubble followed by the contents of both the bathroom and kitchen. From the front bedroom window she could see the house was being completely gutted.

One afternoon early twilight was descending after a day of rain when she reached her front door.

The afternoon had been full of busy hands and cheerful chatter with the Knit and Natter Group. When a little blue van pulled up across the road opposite her a voice vaguely familiar reached her. 'Hello Mrs R, or is it Granny Lane now? Remember me? It's Mitch. We met at the house up the end of the road, near the Pilgrims' Rest Pub. I dropped off the blue table.'

' Oh yes, hello Mitch. I'm Louise to friends, Mrs. R to others and thanks to the local children who walk in the lane I am Granny Lane. I am fine, thanks for asking.'

'You're not by any chance eyeing up my skips are you?' he joked.

'Well, to be truthful, I am actually. I haven't looked today. Being a little on the short side I have been doing a recee from my front bedroom window, up there,' she said pointing.

'Well the men have been clearing the back garden today . You may be lucky. There's an old garden bench to be dumped. Needs work though. Any good?'

'Oh, how wonderful. I need seating in the back. I have a table and four chairs but it isn't enough. We often need six seats and I've got a clever Polish window cleaner who is really brilliant. He can turn his hand to anything.'

'Great. I'll have the men bring it round in a jiffy. Lovely to see you again. Keep well.'

She blinked. In a flash he was gone.
Another Angel to add to her list!

CHAPTER 2

"The courage you need comes from you."

Louise opened her eyes, then instantly, overcome by pain, closed them again. She could hear her heart pounding from her stomach to her ears.

Trying to breathe and trying to be calm she opened her eyes once again, this time, knowing what she would see, and resolved to try and keep them open so that she could sort herself out.

She was half in the hall at the bottom of the stairs, not the right way up but upside-down lying in a crumpled heap, head on the cold tiled floor, one leg crumpled under her and the other lying up the stairs. It could have been only seconds or minutes but it felt like hours when she was woken again by the pain on her left side and the cold unyielding floor on her face.

Knowing her telephone was inaccessible on the bedside table she tried to decide what to do. The umbrella stand stood down the hall filled with umbrellas of all sorts of colours and sizes and a familiar wooden walking stick which had belonged to Jeff's father. Floating in and out of consciousness on the brinks of pain she eased slowly towards the front door. Prepared for battle she waited and waited. From the now overturned umbrella stand she had extracted her battle sword.

Someone would pass eventually she knew and, of course, it was Thursday when she had a routine quick chat with Steve. She knew he would pass in due time pounding the beat in his size 12's. He was not only the community postman but was the community lifesaver too.

Regaining consciousness from one of her pain-filled moments memories of laughter and giggles came to her and visions of characters using Semaphore and Morse Code.

The ...===...===...=== began to be hammered into her brain. The rhythmic banging from the walking stick on the wooden door eventually attracted attention. Steve, Brenda , strange faces and reassuring words hovered around her and in no time it seemed she was being treated in hospital for her injuries which were two breaks in her left arm, a badly bruised hip and a very battered body.

Bad news travels fast they say and so it did. Like Giovanni she met Bernadette and Marie the ward volunteers and she was never short of visitors. The 'girls' from the Knit and Natter group brought grapes and magazines. Pat, leaving the running of the charity shop in charge of her faithful volunteers, came with a book that had been donated that she knew Louise was watching out for. Pete brought a pot of snowdrops which he knew were her favourite flowers and Giovanni flamboyantly showered her with a bunch of flowers from the market stall opposite his cafe window.

They all came, those angels in her life.

School hours and Dan's job prevented the three Musketeer's from visiting the hospital so they sent their hand-made cards via Brenda but it was their surprise to put 'Welcome Home' banners over her door. They were there when Amy and Rachael brought her back home... they were there to settle her in her favourite chair in front of the log fire and.....they were there with mugs of hot chocolate just as she had been for them those years ago.

Back in her cosy home, memories fading, pain suppressed, but imprisoned, a fear overwhelmed her that she would return to the loneliness that she had felt that first Christmas and that was something she could not bear, but with a mantelpiece filled with get-well cards, never short of visitors and phone calls, life started to return to normality.

Pat was the first to bring a parcel to relieve the boredom. It contained a printed tapestry in a frame with all the threads.

'I'm talking from experience. It happened to me once too. You can rest your broken arm on the frame and embroider with the other. Try it and see.'

One Monday afternoon after the weekly session with the 'girls' Brenda popped in with the usual good wishes and was making a cup of tea for Louise when she said, 'On the way here I thought of how lucky I was to have met you. We get on so well don't we?'

' Yes, I think the same. I was beginning to think my decision to downsize to the suburbs was wrong and I was wondering if I should have returned to my roots.'

'Well, I'm glad you chose here, which reminds me I've had this refrain spinning through my head all day. Do you know where it comes from? With that she began to sing: 'People who meet people are the luckiest people in the world.'

'Oh yes, I know it – Barbra Streisand in Funny Girl. I think it was 'need' not meet, but I won't argue with you. Omar Sharif was in it too. I was besotted with him. He was one of my heart-throbs although I was absolutely besotted too with Dirk Bogarde after seeing him in Doctor in the House. I was still in school. I had pictures of him all over my bedroom walls. Did you have a heart-throb too?'

'Me, I had several. Although it was musicals for me. Howard Keel in Seven Brides for Seven Brothers.. That barn raising scene – the dancing and the choreography absolutely stunned me.
I sang and skipped all the way home. The trouble with me was that I fell for all the male leads in any film. My husband always said I was fickle and he was surprised I married him. I didn't tell him that he looked cute like Russ Tamblyn.'

As the weeks passed slowly by they all came, those angels in her life and the healing began.

CHAPTER 3

"Always remember that you are unique, just like everyone else," Margaret Mead.

Louise sensed a tremor in her son's voice when she spoke to him over the phone. Texting was usually his metier and her heart jumped in panic. Luke may have, like his father, chosen the Army as his career but he was no toughie. Occasionally a sensitive side emerged and this seemed to be one such time.

'Mum, do you still have a driving licence?'

'Yes, of course. I use it as my proof of identity. Why?' she answered, sitting down quickly to catch her breath.

'We're swopping the car. It's too small now what with the kids going to after school groups and matches and then there's the scouts and their school bags, sports gear and such like. Then there is always someone's mate to pick up or drop off and the grocery shopping isn't getting any smaller. I know Dad did most of the driving and you haven't driven since Dad passed but you would soon get back into the swing of it. Anyway would you like it?'

Regaining her strength, whilst listening to Luke's garbled form of persuasion, she forced some cheerfulness into her voice and replied, 'That's a lovely thought. A bit of a challenge. Leave it with me for a couple of days, I need to think about it. Is that O.K. Not in a hurry are you?'

'Well, truth is Mum my leave finishes in 10 days so I would like to leave Maria with a replacement and, as you know, we have space for only one vehicle.'

Luke's voice tapering away gave Louise the chance to say, 'Just 24 hours then love, just a day should do it. I promise to ring tomorrow night.'

She slept badly, tossing and turning, with the haunting chant '24 hours, 24 hours' floating through her dreams. Waking suddenly, she sat upright, looked around trying to figure out where she was. Of course, in a sterile hospital space and the doctor was saying, 'We'll know in the next 24 hours.' She closed her eyes and lay back down and when she opened them again she was back in her own bedroom. Jeff had died as a result of that car crash.

Shivering, she pulled the covers upwards over her eyes and the pillow downwards under her chin and tried to sleep but with no success.

She tried another blanket with no success.

With the fear of returning to disturbing dreams, sleep eluding her she knew that delaying her decision was futile so YES she would accept the gift of a car and YES she would learn to drive confidently again, anyway hadn't she always wanted to drive back to the village where she grew up.

At the Knit and Natter group that afternoon she announced, 'Guess what everyone I am getting a car. My son is giving me their old one.'

There was a distinctive pause before anyone spoke and then Brenda, (the Brenda who walked 5 miles each day}, said, 'But none of us have seen you drive, you'll be death on the roads.'

'Oh, come off it, my sister is 85 and she still drives. There's older people than that on the roads,' piped up Elaine.

'Don't worry I'm going to get 'top-up' lessons.'

'Where there's a will there's a way , my Dad always said,' added Pauline supportingly.

That evening a pleased Luke received her positive answer. It wasn't long before chance once again knocked on her door in the form of a Council-run Road Show for older pedestrians and drivers. Curiousity and the temptation of refreshments on arrival and a buffet lunch brought all her friends together in one place and it wasn't long before their table, between talks from the Police, Council and Transport Authorities, was covered with leaflets and freebies, (pens, key-rings and such like) but for Louise she was now the proud holder of a leaflets from local Driving Schools and another setting out the services of a leading U.K. Road Safety Charity. This charity, based in the United Kingdom and run by volunteers, aimed to improve driving. They advocated helping driving skills through courses and coaching,

'This is it girls,' she said excitedly, 'This is it. I've found my next challenge.'

CHAPTER 4
"Do foolish things but do them with enthusiasm."

Looking back over the past two years it was inevitable that circumstances would push her in the next direction. The next push, in fact, came in the form of a telephone conversation with her cousin Fiona in Scotland.

They had grown up together in a small village in the countryside, attended the same schools, in the same year. She had been a bridesmaid at Fiona and Stuart's wedding and a very pregnant Fiona had been Matron-of-Honour when she and Jeff married a few years later. Over the years, letters and photographs had flown between the two homes and now they spoke frequently on the phone.

'Have you had a letter from Willie McCloud yet? You remember him of course. He latched on to you in Kindergarden and followed you around like a lapdog in Juniors. He was always pulling your pigtails and still fancied you in Senior School. I'm sure you remember him, anyway he and his wife Irene (I don't think you know her, she's lovely) are organising a school pals reunion. You must come. It'll be fun, catching up with old pals (literally old now, of course). We can put you up. Both of ours, like yours, have flown the nest now and their rooms rarely get used. Not many of us left who stayed local so we need your support.'

'What a brilliant idea. The letter hasn't come yet. I look forward to getting it. Of course I'll come.'

She would drive, naturally, and use her newfound skills. For the first time in her life she would drive, alone, a long distance and she would wear her tartan dress kilt, which had, for many years, been packed away in the profusion of packages in the back bedroom.

One particularly rainy day found her in that cluttered domain, lifting and shifting neatly labelled boxes, one of which, particularly heavy, had lost its label. To her delight it contained her old portable typewriter, used so much during her university days. She had typed her dissertations of 10,000 words each on it and those of several of her friends to earn much needed money. Looking back she had been grateful for her parents' insistence that she take a typing course after leaving school during the lull before going to university.
Her well-learnt talent was used to earn money too in temporary jobs.

Taking it, and her precious kilt, downstairs to the kitchen a thrill of excitement filled her. Having no typing paper she inserted a piece of business mail with an unused reverse side and began to type. Within minutes her dancing fingers, exercised by her newfound hobbies, were tempting her into drawing a story.

My name is Louise Rydal . The local children call me Granny Lane.....

98765432 23456789 What shall I type now?

The fox jumped over the lazy stile. No. The lazy fox jumped over the stile.

This is fun....trewqpoiuy theiwlsidkrmfng

It had been a long time since she had written poems and stories, since university days in fact. Work, marriage and children had brought pressures on her life, but now, the urge repossessed her and she joined a creative writers' group in the city. From that day on stories, poetry and prose poured out of her, some at the most unexpected times.

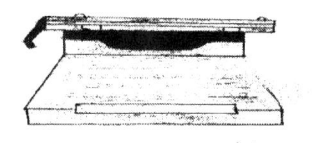

CHAPTER 5
"Hold your nerve, the storm will pass."

A military maneouvre couldn't have been planned with more precision.

Arranged for the last week-end in November, Luke had set out daily distances for her drive, (in view of her age and 'learner' status,) and suitable hotels, (again for a woman of her circumstances) Who is he kidding, he meant age!

Winter had spread its blanket over the land but stubborn remnants of late Autumn remained. Lone hardened leaves were still clinging to bowed wizened branches . Here and there a flaming bush, protected by a stalwart wall or tolerant trees remained. In towns mushy burnished rugs still blocked gutters and gullies and when she drove further north, the moors displayed their carpets of purple heather. Arriving in the arms of her cousin, the adventure continued with her favourite tipple, a single malt whisky liqueur.

The next few days, duly forewarned by Irene, a motley band were thrown into a programme of walks around historic sites, museums, tourist attractions and a tour and tasting in a Whisky Distillery, ensuring that those, like Louise, who had roamed from their childhood home would renew their memories of their heritage from the smell of the heather, the taste of so many different foods, the warm burr of an ancient language on the voices they heard and, on one occasion, the sound of distant haunting pipes.

Irene slipped into a seat beside her when they were all in a cafe adjoining the Museum.

'It's cosy in here isn't it? Are you enjoying the trips? Not over-exercising you are we? Fiona told me that you had a nasty fall earlier in the year.'

'Oh, thanks for asking. I am fine now. I stupidly ignored the fact that a pair of slippers were getting old. I have been building myself up for this by exercising every day. I'm loving the outings that you've planned. I must admit it takes me back and I've loved learning all about heather in this place. Did you know that almost all of the plant can be used, from brooms to medicine? It's all been wonderful.'

'I must admit I have learnt a lot too. Glad you're enjoying everything.'

The evening of the school reunion dinner started with a storm. Guests arrived damp and bedraggled but once in the reception of the hotel, the wooden panelled walls adorned with ancient antlers and tartan patterned carpet raised their spirits.

Shaking themselves dry by a roaring log fire, within minutes they were greeted by their host, a vision of swinging kilt accompanied by a booming voice bounding towards them.

'Louisey, Louisey, ma wee lassie, welcome home,' shouted Willie, sliding a heavy arm across her shoulders and planting a kiss on her lips.

Horrified, she extricated herself from his overpowering embrace, forcing a smile, said briskly, 'Well hello to you too, still the same old Willie I see.'

A highland piper welcomed all the guests into dinner, a traditional meal of haggis, venison and cranachan. Speeches followed, then the ceilidh. For some, not inclined to exercise it was a chance to mingle with old friends in an atmosphere of swirling kilts, a riot of tartans and joviality.

All in all the return to Scotland was a poignant time for many, Louise included, and it led to an unexpected outburst of her creative skills. During a quiet time, taking the air and gazing out into the floodlit garden, a 'thank-you' poem for Irene emerged.

Ode to Irene

You are the green of the glens
And the depth of the deepest loch.
You are the height of the mountains
And as precious as each tiny rock.
You have chosen the ways we have travelled
Been our leader, guide and friend.
Over moor, mountain and valley we've wandered
And we really don't want it to end.
History and culture we've encountered
Some Haggis, Venison and Cranachan have tried.
At storms and floods we've not floundered
We're glad we came along for the ride.
But good times must slip into our memory banks
And with them we give you our love and our thanks.

Leaving was bitter-sweet.

'Don't leave it so long before you come again,' pleaded Fiona.

'I won't The trip has made me realise how much I have been homesick. I could never have been one of those people who bravely emigrated. England is far enough.'

'Take care, it's right dreich.'

'I will,' shouted Louise, as she turned the wheels towards home.

Granny Lane's World Collapses

CHAPTER 1
"A bit of a struggle is good for the soul."

Drawn into Christmas once again, it proved a time of reflection. It was accepted that there would always be changes. Alisha and Ali's store had expanded into the next-door shop and they talked of expanding their family too which pleased Alisha's mother. Giovanni now had permission to put tables outside his shop which had been such a success that he employed a chef and provided meals. All her family, friends and neighbours were closely woven into the fabric of her life.

Wild winter weather heralded in the new year. Gale force winds causing damage and floods swept across the country. Names, which were often given to human beings, were given to these storms in alphabetical order. It didn't help that particular name could be that of someone you knew, especially if they were of a pleasant nature. Mind you, if the name corresponded to someone like an overbearing school bully of the past, then it was aptly used.

Joining Brenda to walk to the Pilgrims' Rest Pub where the Knit and Natter group now met, having outgrown the little back room at the coffee shop which had now extended it's premises, they linked arms to steady each other against the blasts. Ever optimistic, Louise panted, 'Roll on Springtime. I'm getting too old for this!'

'Thank goodness we have a roof over our heads and friendship, as well as all the things we do,' answered Brenda, trying to avoid a large puddle.

'Yes, I am so lucky. My eyes, ears and teeth are going but I'm still here,' joked Louise pulling her hat on tighter and squeezing her friend's arm. 'This year is going to be a good year. I've got a holiday to Italy booked, Thomas and Molly get married in the Autumn and Jacob's wife and girls are due to join him in the home he has prepared for them. He is so excited and I am looking forward to meeting them.'

For Louise, March the 15th changed everything. She knew the date well for it was ingrained on her mind and heart. It was the day she went into 'lockdown' as it was officially called.

The Coronavirus Pandemic, or Covid 19, had crept across the world, invaded England's shores, encroached on her city and now resided in her community, changing the daily life of everyone in it. She surprised herself by entering into the restrictions willingly, at first, then, after three weeks, felt devastated.

Alone, once again, she was lonely, with no prospect of returning to the contented well run world she had come to love. The lane that had shared it's name with her was now quiet, the stainless-steel table no longer offering morsels of friendship.

To begin with, like the rest of the world, life was dominated by the media with stories of struggle, death and forecasts of worsening conditions, then reports of scarcities. Because of her age and health, she had been labelled as being amongst the most vulnerable, therefore advised to allow someone to do the shopping and the role of 'chief shopper' became that of Dan, next door.

Solitude wrapped it's arms around her, crushing her spirit. It was on the third Sunday that she was shocked into reality. The doorbell rang, followed by a cheerful knock. Opening it she found her daughter, Amy, standing a short distance away.

'I'll not come in, Mum, Want to keep to the rules and anyway Rachael works on the Covid wards so we must be careful. Just popped over to see if you are O.K. and bring some treats.'

Noticing the tears rise in her Mother's eyes, she continued, 'You're not Mum are you? You're not O.K. are you I mean. You'll have to go out for a walk each day. You are allowed to. Go down the lane or pop over the road to the park. Walking will make you feel better. Promise me Mum. Start tomorrow.' Holding back the tears, Louise assured Amy that she would take a daily walk, perhaps starting right away and closed the door to face, once again, the prison walls.

Louise stepped tentatively out of her front door as if a prisoner released on parole. The sun was shining! What was the sun doing? Should it be allowed to shine whilst all it's worshippers were trapped under the shadow of a pandemic. The road was quiet. She walked warily down a tree-lined side street. Had she got the time right?

Was it really Sunday afternoon. It was so quiet that it felt as if it was just past dawn. She blinked her eyes, now welling up with heavy tears, then slipped through an almost hidden green, anti-vandal-painted gate into her small local park which was all that was left of a once stately hall and estate. Her spirits rose, the waiting tears receded as her footsteps took energy from the waiting springy verdure.

As she stood surveying the view around her the poem formed. It came quickly and she let the rhyme ripple through her. The walk was short but profitable as it raised her spirits and produced an unexpected result. She hurried home, flung off her coat and started to type......

The Caged Bird

It was Sunday, the third in isolation alone,
I broke the ban and set off to walk a few yards from my home.
I hoped that in the park I would find some peace of mind.
If not that, then some respite of some other kind.
There were no cars, no walkers in the once noisy street.
Pavements were no longer paced by busy rushing feet.
The grass was fresh and green and sprinkled with the morning dew.
'Look at us, look at us,' said the celandines and the daisies too.
Swaying gently in the breeze stood Wordsworth's daffodils.
Wishing me, standing there, a feeling of goodwill.
Swings and roundabouts no longer held children at their play.
The sounds of running and excited feet no longer filled each day.

Instead the birds replaced those missing sounds with their vocal treat.

They lifted my weary heart and put fresh springs beneath my feet.

I saw the trees in blossom and silken buds just bursting through,

And I knew that one day nature would our precious world renew.

As I left the park blue speedwell sped me on my way,

And this flightless bird had been released to fly another day.

CHAPTER 2
"Love is like a vine, if you don't tend it you will lose it."

Walking, not every day at first, gradually became the norm. Walking had been part of her life, from childhood and through marriage so starting again seemed a normal course to follow. With it, came the habit of knocking on doors, which she found both uplifting for herself and, she was told, for that of her chosen friends too.

It was Brenda who became her 'Monday visit' at the end of her walk. They would stand,(at the designated 2 metres apart of course) at Brenda's front door and commiserate over their situation and of the trials and tribulations of life. Brenda was the first person she confided in about the poem.

'I'd love to see it,' enthused Brenda, not surprised that Louise would come up with something new. 'You're so clever. I can't do things like that.'

'Don't belittle yourself. You are absolutely brilliant at knitting and crochet. All that Aran and Fairisle you do and I remember that fantastic playmat you made for your Grandson, with roads and little cars and houses.

I certainly couldn't do things like that. Everyone has a talent I've found. Perhaps they don't always know what it is. That's certainly yours as well as other things you do, like being a good friend. Which reminds me, I have some time on my hands. Ha, ha, would you believe it! As well as time I have some odd balls of wool I picked up before the lockdown and I could use an easy way of using them up.'

Brenda replied 'I have just the thing. A pattern for knitted jackets and bonnets for prem babies. Just the thing for you. I'll write out the patterns, dead easy ones. That'll keep you busy and they will be gladly accepted at the Women's.'

'That's great. Give me a ring and I'll collect them.'

The 'Wednesday visit' was Pat. Poor Pat, who had been furloughed from her job at the charity shop and who had not only helped with the old cash machine but had, more recently, taught her how to manage the complexities (for that was what they were) of the new Smart Phone her daughter had encouraged her to buy.

When hearing of her poem, Pat said, 'Oh, how wonderful. You must bring it round and I'll photocopy it for you. Tell me how many copies you want. I'm sure it will give people pleasure.

Your calling helps by the way. Thanks for that. You are so brave, going out I mean. I'm too scared.'

Turning away from Pat's doorway she noticed the roses flowering over the doorway opposite and her mind went into unexpected creative mode once again.

The Challenge

What will happen when we step beyond these prison walls?

Will we worry that with each step a danger will enfold?

Life, not quite the same, we surely must expect to meet.

Take courage, take that step and walk into the street.

Your neighbours' gardens will be a bright and cheerful sight,

Clematis and magnolias have blossomed overnight.

Lilacs, cherries and bluebells then come into view.

And see that rose climbing over the door of number 2.

Nature has been working without us you will find.

Keep walking, carry on and do not look behind.

Dandelions are popping up in every crevice, crack and lawn.

Each tree is putting forth new growth of its very own.

May is out, so there is no doubt that Spring is on its way.

So put spring in your step too and challenge each new day.

As signs of Spring appeared the old Granny Lane could be seen in her garden by the more frequent passers-by in the lane but they were no longer offered refreshment.

Her silver bob, now shoulder length, could be seen tied back with a bright ribbon from a Christmas chocolate box (with the name of the confectioner running through it) or topped with a sunhat – a hat which would not now be taken on holiday due to the cancellation of all travel. She had taken a holiday alone every year since her husband's death. She had started with a coach holiday in England and despite on occasion, feeling lonely and, she confessed, it hadn't been easy avoiding wary wives who thought their husbands would be in danger of being lured away by an attractive widow, had advanced to organised holidays abroad. It was not the loss of a holiday which pained her now, but her daughter's distress. She was, as an Air Steward unemployed, as were so many in the Aviation Business. Amy, her restless daughter, who was used to flying around the world was now trapped like an exotic bird in a golden cage. As for herself, she would take matters into her own hands. Due to fly away to the Italian lakes on the 13th May she planned, with her usual sense of humour, her next challenge, and to record it in diary form.

My SAGA Covitalian Holiday. May 2020

Reflections of the Italian Lakes

Dear Diary DAY 1

This morning the BBC showed us how booking in would be done in the future at an Airport, under strict social distancing with masks and gloves. At least the two magpies fighting for a titbit on my lawn could fly off to other domains. Lucky birds!

I'm going to learn an Italian word or phrase each day: Buon giorno (Good morning, good evening, good night) is today's, Perhaps if I say it often enough I'll think I am in Italy.

It took a while to get into the holiday mood. Choice of clothes seemed to help. My recently bought T-shirt is lovely.

Lunch was Bruschettine topped with tomato and basil and a drizzle of extra virgin olive oil. Dinner was a wood fired pizza topped with Italian fennel salami, tomatoes and parsley and Mozzarella cheese.

Dear Diary DAY 2

The Hotel L'Approdo is lovely. Set right beside the Lake Orta with views of the mountains, it was to be our base for two days. I should have been exploring the lake by boat so not to be outdone I collected my daily 6,000 steps in a park a 20 minute walk from my home, with a pretty little lake. Today I am wearing my new holiday shoes. They are great. I feel like I am walking on air. Today's word: Grazie (Thank you)

Temperature is 11 degrees Celsius here. It's not much better in Italy.

Lunch was Bruschetta made from toasted sourdough with a topping made of red onion, cannellini beans, lemon juice and fresh parsley. Dinner was Chicken Arrabbiata.

Dear Diary DAY 3

A day of leisure was planned and a trip to the quaint Umbrella Museum which because of the restrictions was closed. Spent the day washing and cleaning. The word for today is: per favore (please) But, lunch was delicious – a Mediterranean vegetable and pesto focaccia and dinner was a favourite I often cooked for myself, Macaroni and Tuna Fish Layer.

Dear Diary DAY 4

The Hotel Simplon, on the shores of Lake Maggiore, is family owned. This pretty pink building, enveloped by Mediterranean gardens is an easy distance of 0,4 km. from the ferry. Plenty of walking expected to match my daily challenge of 6,000 steps. Decorated in traditional Italian style, the decor of the hotel is awe inspiring, giving a very Art Deco style.

Lunch was Bruschetta with tomato, basil and Feta. Dinner was Gino's Traditional Italian Peasants' Soup, a meal in itself. I sat in the sunny kitchen window as I ate it wearing a summer holiday loose cotton dress. My word of the day: Scusi (sorry).

Dear Diary DAY 5

According to the news I am allowed to drive, at last, to a beauty spot to meet a friend, 2 metres apart, of course, so instead of beautiful Locarno it was to a large Victorian park on the south side of town. Locarno, founded in the 12th century at the base of the Alps has too many attractions to list here and the included trip on the Centovalli Scenic Railway [meaning 100 valleys] is said to be an unique train journey. I wore my favourite sun hat, years old it is often admired (thanks M & S) and sat on a blanket on the grass. I had salad from a lunchbox.... va bene, the word for 'that's nice' is appropriate here I think. Dinner was a Lasagne and a beautiful salad.

Dear Diary DAY 6

The nearest I could get to the immaculate gardens of Villa Taranto is my local park which is about a five minute walk from my house.

It was a life-saver for me after three weeks of complete lockdown. I wrote a poem there, the first of three. It is even prettier now with its borders of forget-me-nots and tulips as well as two beautiful golden sweet-smelling Azaleas.

Lunch was home-made Tomato and Basil Soup and dinner was a basic Tuna Pasta. The phrase of the day was: Non bevo/non fumo (I don't drink/smoke). I gave up wearing summer clothes. It may be 23 degrees Celsius in Italy but I'm back into a thermal vest, sweater and jeans....

Dear Diary DAY 7

The Palace Hotel, Citta, sits a two kilometre walk from the shores of Lake Garda, sits in a tranquil location in the beautiful panoramic town of Arco. Wore my pale blue pleated trousers and delicate white top to remind myself of the (now cancelled) visit to the silk production town of Como which is closely linked to the fashion houses of Milan and New York. I am now addicted to Bruschettine which I had for lunch again and Dinner was Pesce al Cartoccio [fish baked in foil with herbs]. Naturally the word for today is: ottimo (excellent).

Dear Diary DAY 8

Rain in Italy but warmer here. Makes me feel better. Watched a film based in Rome – a romance. Should have been on a scenic drive. Pigged out on Focaccia for lunch and had a Pizza Margherita for dinner. Today's phrase is: Mi chiamo (my name is).

Dear Diary DAY 9

Scusi diary. Buon giorno everyone. Bear with me per favour. Non parlo italiano (I don't speak Italian). Watched something on catch-up T.V. about the lives of Venitian painters.

Is desperation setting in? Rain in Italy – back in summer clothes here in England. Lunch is Tomato and Red Pepper Soup with sourdough and dinner is the second half of my Macaroni and Tuna Layer.

Dear Diary DAY 10

The last hotel, The Hotel Ariston. a family run hotel in a fantastic location rich in tradition and beauty with the lake only 0.09 miles away. I sat in a friend's garden by a large pool listening to cascading water, watching basking carp and talking in the beauty of vibrant yellow iris. For a moment I was transported to Italy.

Lunch was a cheese and tomato toastie and dinner was Spagetti and Meat Balls. Como si chiama? (what is your name?) chosen just in case I meet a tall, dark stranger. Mind you, on reflection a medium-height, grey-haired stranger will do!

Dear Diary DAYS 11,12, and 13

Days roll into nothingness during this lockdown. When we should have been soaking up sun, beauty and culture in Italy, here in England we are being battered by 50-60 mph winds which are creating havoc in gardens, parks and woodlands. My final meal was: King Prawn Alfredo, Tiromisu with Vino Bianco and my words are: Vorrei (I'd like), La Torta (cake) and La lista dei vini (wine list). I imagine, that at this point, my chosen vocabulary is becoming of some use.

Dear Diary DAY 14

ARRIVEDERCI ITALY (Goodbye Italy)

My thanks to:

My daughter for doing the shopping.

M & S and Tesco for the lovely food and drink.

My summer wardrobe for keeping me sane.

My trusty typewriter.

Last, but not least, my travel agent and my SAGA holiday brochure.

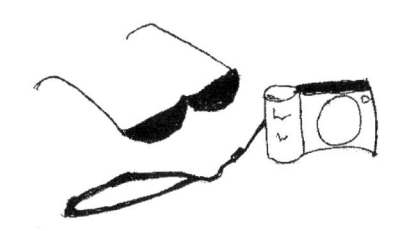

CHAPTER 3

"Don't float through life, make some waves."

Had the holiday really happened, then returning back to England she would have been thrown into the path of another storm, this time with a foreign name that had no connection to anyone in her life.

More like Autumn than Spring, leaves, branches and twigs raced, cannonballed, and flew down the road, quickly finding respite in gutters, behind flower pots and under hedges. The trees in the distance that she had noticed that first Christmas from her front room window, were now bending drunkenly.

A strange noise attracted her to the front door and she opened it to find Dan taking groceries from the boot of his car, at the same time two objects emerged from under the front bumper, almost floating in the wind, being chased by two excited children – Oceane and Louis. They returned, each carrying a strange object.

'Hello Granny Lane. Did you see that? Our Ecobricks blew down the road,' panted Louis.

'Well, I did see you running. It looked fun. What are Ecobricks? I am showing my age I'm afraid.'

'You're not, not old I mean. You can't know everything. They are plastic bottles filled with rubbish plastic and stuff. Daddy says we are helping to save the environment. They are making walls in our playground at school with them. They look great.'

'How clever and interesting. Perhaps I will see the finished walls one day.'

'Off you go inside young man. Mrs. R will catch her death of cold standing there,' interrupted Dan placing her groceries on the door step.

'Oh Dan, thanks for being my main shopper. I am so grateful. I wish I could do something for you in return.'

'It's nothing Mrs. R, I do most of mine online but I still have to pick up the odd item. You could do something for me though. Actually it's the ironing. I am hopeless at it and now with the children homeschooling and me working from home, I just can't seem to cope. Not that we heed to iron everything after all nobody would see us, anyway, we seem to spend all day sometimes in our P.J's and bedsocks.'

'Of course I'll do it Dan. No problem. Leave it with me whenever you want. Can't have you taking the children walking in the park for exercise looking scruffy can we? You need to look decent and keep up standards. It reminds me of the time when I had a neighbour who, every school day, took her children to school in a taxi wearing her pyjamas and mock fur coat, wearing those fancy boots. I can't think of the name – oh yes, moon boots I think. Anyway all the neighbours were talking about her. Anyway you might bump into a nice young lady. There's still time yet, you know, you're still a young man.' 'No chance Mrs. R, nobody would take me on with two kids,' laughed Dan, turning away.

'We'll see, we'll see. Thanks once again and give my love to the kids.' And with that she closed the door remembering the wedding invitation on the fridge door. Because of the pandemic Thomas and Molly's wedding plans had to be put on hold. Summer came along with lessening restrictions but life didn't return to normal. Face masks, hand washing and social distancing prevailed and were to become the norm. It was on a particularly pleasant summer's day that the third of her poems made an appearance to make her Covid-Trilogy as she named them.

The Covid-blues

I clean, I polish and dust each day,
The dishes get washed and tidied away.

The garden is weeded and hedges cut
I have even started a vegetable plot.

For the next meal I cannot wait.
The tray is ready with knife, fork and plate,

We may not go back to the way we were
So of that 'new normal' we must be aware.

To all the rules you must closely attend,
You must not stand close to your friend.

And when you travel on train or bus
A mask you must wear without a fuss.

Try anything to stop these covid-blues.
Your sense of humour you must not lose.

Try doing the things your mother did,
Do the things you did when you were a kid.

Try new foods, learn new tasks,
And keep a smile behind those masks.

Learn new ways to still keep fit
BUT Follow the rules and do your bit.

CHAPTER 4

"If you want rainbows, then please accept the rain."

... and turned towards home... The typewriter fell silent. Louise pulled the sheet of words out of the rollers with a flick, pleased with her efforts which she knew would give pleasure and, she hoped, amuse the small group that had become her readers.

HARD TIMES

I woke up scared. The sun was climbing into a clear blue pond scoured clean by the spears and torrents of the night's electric storm.

Actually I was not so much scared as worried. It was the day of my annual check-up. I had noticed changes and had hoped that my mother had not noticed them too. Firstly let me explain, she isn't my mother but she calls me her 'Baby' and I like it. She feeds me and makes sure that I look good despite my years.

She too seemed a little concerned as she left me and made her way to the waiting-room, not before she had given me a gentle pat and a departing reassuring word.

The news was not good. Mother took it well to my surprise. Back home my spirits slumped. I was scared and worried once again, this time scared of what the future would bring. Time moved at a snail's pace. Then, there she was armed for battle. The day was hot, one of the hottest of the summer. The journey took us through unfamiliar territory, far from my smart suburban home with its gardens and parks, to a strange run-down looking building and there she left me.

My heart was broken but time passed. The treatment was harsh, painful at times but I made friends with Daisy, Red and Bumper. They called me Jazz. Then she was there, my mother I mean. I heard her voice at first and then my spirits soared and I tried to look pleased to see her. As we started the journey back home she put her hand on the piece of paper on the seat beside her on which was printed M.O.T. Test Certificate and said, 'Well, my Baby, another year together, let's enjoy it.'

She waved to John, the mechanic, and eased out of the garage into the busy traffic and turned towards home. THE END

It amused her to wonder how far her readers would get before they realised the subject speaking was a car. In fact her car had failed the M.O.T. and had to be repaired immediately. She had taken it to a garage recommended by one of Luke's school friends. The whole experience had been quite emotional in such different times but she was grateful it led to the creation of her next piece of work.

It was Amy's voice on the phone this time that caused her to sit down quickly at the kitchen table. It was a tremulous, tear filled voice.

'Mum, oh Mum. It's Rachael. She's got Covid. She's in Intensive Care. They won't let me see her. I don't know what to do.'

'Oh no,' replied Louise, at first stunned, unable to say anything. 'I'm coming over to you. Meet me in the little park, next to the Retail Park. Give me 30 minutes.' Once again she was thankful that she had returned to driving.

At the sight of her daughter, waiting at the entrance to the car park, her heart sank. Shoulders sagging, devoid of make-up, she was wrapped in a coat, a coat that was obviously not her size but Rachael's.

Unable to wrap her arms and body around her daughter and hold her tightly to her Louise felt her heart break. They sat at each end of a cold metal park bench and wept uncontrollably.

Sadly the worst happened.

The Coronavirus was coming too close to home. First Rachael, then news of Steve's dad, who thankfully was now on the road to recovery, and then sadly, Oceane and Louis' Grand'mère in France died. Having lost their own mother and now her mother, their Grand'mère, life seemed so unfair. Her heart bled for them but what was worse she couldn't give them the cuddle they both needed.

All she could do, she decided, was to help her friends and neighbours with little gestures and put her love into knitting tiny garments – the pile grew and grew.

Cap-sleeved Cardi and Hat for Prem Babies

DK yarn 50 gram ball. No. 8/4mm needles. 1 button.

Worked in one piece in Garter Stitch [All rows knit]

CARDI : Cast on 40 stitches and knit 2 rows.

Increase row: Knit 2 sts. Inc. In next st. Knit to last 3 sts, inc. in next st. K2.

Repeat increase row until 60 sts. on needle. Work 16 rows straight.

Buttonhole row: K2, yarn forward, K2tog. Knit to end of row.

Divide for back and fronts: Knit to last 16 sts. [slip these onto stitch holder]. Cast on 5 sts. at beginning of next row [for sleeve] . Knit these 5 sts. and across row until last 16 sts. [slip these onto stitch holder]

Cast on 5 sts. at beginning of next row. Knit these 5 sts. and across row until end. [38 sts.]

Knit 20 rows. Cast off loosely.

Work fronts: ** Put 16 sts. on needle. Join yarn. Cast on 5 sts. Knit these and rest of row.

Front edge decrease row: K2, k2tog., knit to end of row. Knit 1 row.

Repeat these 2 rows until 12 sts. remain. Cast off loosely for shoulders. **

Repeat from ** to ** for other front.

Join shoulder and under-arm seams. Sew on button.

HAT: Cast on 48 sts. and work 5 rows in k1. P1 rib. Work 12 rows in Garter Stitch.

Next row: K2tog. across row. [24 sts.]

Next row: Knit.

Next row: K2tog. across row. [12 sts.]

Next row: Knit.

Next row: K2tog. across row. [6 sts.]

Next row: Knit.

Cut yarn long enough to sew down seam and pull through stitches. Sew seam

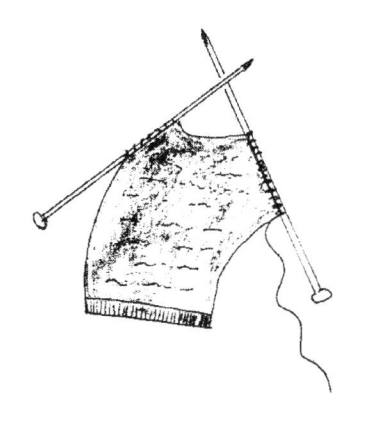

CHAPTER 5
"Whoever is happy will make others happy too." Anne Frank.

'I think I am going mad,' Louise jokingly confided in Fiona a few weeks before Christmas. 'I've lost a day so missed taking a tablet, burnt a pan of onions I was softening for soup then knocked it on the floor and chipped a tile. As well as that I've bought a real Christmas tree, with roots after always having an artificial one all my life. I'm sure Amy, who got it for me, thinks I'm going mad too.'

Fiona laughed, 'I'm pretty sure you're not. Stuart said only the other day that I was doing similar things. I've laundered the same bed linen twice in five days and I threw his newspaper into the recycling bin before he had even opened it. He says he's looking for an Old Peoples' Home for me. Ha ha. No chance!'

'The stupid thing is, I no longer had tree decorations so I made six angels and decided to do what the Americans do, string some popcorn. Well, have you ever done popcorn? (Fiona tried to interrupt with a 'yes' at this point but with no luck) So being a microwave fan I had a go.

Got Dan to get me a packet. What fun I had. It didn't work at first but I got the hang of it eventually but then found the stringing up a bit of a messy job. You need a sharp needle and patience. Good job I didn't get sugar-coated, otherwise I would have eaten them all.'

Silently, day by day, long night by night, Christmas, under expected restrictions, arrived and she found herself alone just like that first Christmas, but not lonely.

The day was well planned, breakfast, phone calls to and from family and friends, and a light lunch followed by the Queen's Speech. For later she had chosen a frozen meal to be heated in the microwave and an evening in front of the television watching her favourite programmes on 'catch-up'.

It was the sun that teased her and tempted her to take a walk. The air was crisp and fresh. The lane was quiet. Walking further than she intended she reached the river which always seemed to fascinate her. This time it was swollen, dangerously racing to the sea.

Returning home, kicking off her walking boots, she picked them up to place in the cupboard under the stairs, and the typewriter caught her eye.
The black, uninteresting box, once opened, like

Pandora's Box, had been a good friend. She talked to it a lot, after all it had become a constant companion. Together they had produced lots of work lately, short stories, prose and poetry and some letters as, much to her regret, her handwriting was losing its steadiness. Picking it up and placing it on the kitchen table, she said, 'Here we go again, my friend. I've got another one for you ………'

<u>Horizons</u>

Will I ever see the sea again
Or walk along a coastal path,
See the city on the skyline
Where all my life I've passed?
Will I ever see the places
That have meant so much to me,
Or will I in this foreign land
Stay, for all eternity.
Will I return to the land of my birth
To touch and smell the blood-red earth.
Will I breathe the fresh air of Spring
Or see the glossomer of a dragonfly's wing?

I must be inspired by those
Who, have trod this soil before me,
Lift up my hand, take paper and pen
Write words, make stories once again.
My walls will become wider
From the world I will not hide,
For healing comes not from solitude
But from something deep inside.
I will see the sea again and walk the coastal path,
See the city on the skyline, when all this bitterness has passed…

Twilight descending, the act of drawing the curtains heralded her planned evening. By-passing her usual chair she stretched herself out on the settee and cuddled under her new electric heated throw (a family present of course) and reached for the new book her little extended family next door had given her. For a moment she closed her eyes and suddenly a thought came to her...

Perhaps it was time now, to write a story. A story maybe about a little Grandmother, her adventures and the people she met on the way. She would have to think of a title of course.

Her eyelids fluttered momentarily and in that warm cosy room the unopened book slid silently to the floor.

Acknowledgement

My sincere thanks to Kevin Roach of Beatles Liverpool and More Ltd., for his patience, advice and valued help in the preparation of this, my debut book.

June Soo. May 2021